Centerville Library
Washington-Centerville Public Librar
Centerville, Ohio

DISCARD

W9-CLD-360

SEEDS

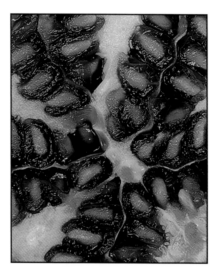

BLACKBIRCH PRESS

An imprint of Thomson Gale, a part of The Thomson Corporation

Detroit • New York • San Francisco • San Diego • New Haven, Conn. • Waterville, Maine • London • Munich

Consultant: Kimi Hosoume
Associate Director of GEMS (Great
  Explorations in Math and Science),
Director of PEACHES (Primary
  Explorations for Adults, Children,
  and Educators in Science),
Lawrence Hall of Science,
University of California,
Berkeley, California

For The Brown Reference Group plc
Editors: John Farndon and Angela Koo
Picture Researcher: Clare Newman
Design Manager: Lynne Ross
Managing Editor: Bridget Giles
Children's Publisher: Anne O'Daly
Production Director: Alastair Gourlay
Editorial Director: Lindsey Lowe

© 2006 The Brown Reference Group plc.
First published by Thomson Gale, a part
of the Thomson Corporation.

Thomson, Star Logo and Thorndike are trademarks and Gale and Blackbirch Press
are registered trademarks used herein under license.

For more information, contact
Blackbirch Press
27500 Drake Rd.
Farmington Hills, MI 48331-3535
Or you can visit our Internet site at http://www.gale.com

ALL RIGHTS RESERVED.
No part of this work covered by the copyright hereon may be reproduced or used in
any form or by any means—graphic, electronic, or mechanical, including photocopying,
recording, taping, Web distribution or information storage retrieval systems—without
the written permission of the copyright owner.

Every effort has been made to trace the owners of copyrighted material.

PHOTOGRAPHIC CREDITS
Corbis: Dennis Blachut 20, Neil Miller/Papilio 16, Kevin Schafer 13, Phil Schermeister 9t;
Corbis Royalty Free: 18/19; **FLPA:** Mark Moffett/Minden Pictures 17; **NHPA:** Ernie James 12;
Photolibrary.com: Harold Taylor 11, Stephen Wisbauer/Botanica 10; **Photos.com:** 1, 4, 7t, 8/9,
19tr, 21, 22; **Still Pictures:** Thomas D. Mangelsen 15, Jochen Tack 3b, 5.

Front cover: Photos.com

LIBRARY OF CONGRESS CATALOGING-IN-PUBLICATION DATA

Farndon, John.
  Seeds / by John Farndon.
    p. cm. — (World of plants)
  Includes bibliographical references and index.
  ISBN 1-4103-0419-1 (lib. : alk. paper)
  1. Seeds (Botany)—Juvenile literature. I. Title

  QK661.F37 2005
  575.6'8—dc22

                                                              2005047047

Printed and bound in Thailand
10 9 8 7 6 5 4 3 2 1

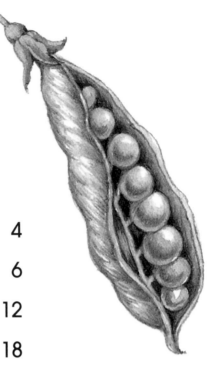

Contents

Seeds and plants

Nearly every plant begins life as a tiny seed. The seed grows into a plant that one day makes its own seeds.

▼ Acorns

Acorns on an oak tree are nuts. Each acorn holds a seed that can grow into an oak tree.

Seeds are amazing little packages. They are a complete starter kit, holding all that is needed to grow a new plant. Inside every seed, there is a tiny plant, with a baby root and stem.

This tiny plant is called an embryo, just like a new baby person inside a mother. The seed has a store of food, too. This helps the plant when it is ready to grow. Some seeds, like beans, are nearly all food. Each seed also has a tough coat that protects it from harm.

Plants make seeds inside a part of the plant called a fruit. People eat fleshy fruits, such as oranges. Inside an orange are many small seeds. But there are other kinds of fruits. Pea pods are dry fruits. Nuts are dry, hard fruits.

It's Amazing!

The biggest seeds of all belong to a palm tree called the coco de mer. The coco de mer lives mostly on the warm islands of the Seychelles in the Indian Ocean. It grows a giant hard fruit a bit like a coconut. The fruit has a tough shell or husk. Inside the husk is a seed almost as big as the fruit. A coco de mer seed can weigh up to 50 pounds (20 kilograms)!

5

A tough husk holds the seed.

▶ **Coco de mer**
A coco de mer is about twice as big as a pumpkin.

The husk splits here as the plant grows.

All about seeds

Seeds come in all shapes, sizes, and colors. Some are as big as a fist. Some are so small they look like dust.

Different plants make different numbers of seeds. A palm tree makes just a few very big seeds. Each of these is a coconut. Orchid flowers make millions of very tiny seeds. Orchid seeds are so tiny that a teaspoon could hold more than a million seeds!

Not every seed made by a plant grows into another plant. An oak tree makes 90,000 acorns. Each one contains a seed. Yet fewer than a hundred of these seeds grow into oak trees. Most acorns are eaten by animals or land somewhere oaks cannot grow.

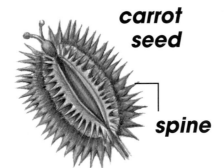

carrot seed

spine

hazelnut

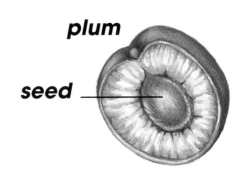

plum

seed

Different seeds

A carrot seed has tiny spines. Inside a hazelnut is a seed. The seed of a plum is the pit inside the fruit. Peas, foxglove flowers, and shepherd's purse plants have seeds in pods.

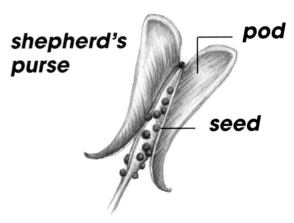

shepherd's purse

pod

seed

Although many acorns are lost, the oak tree makes lots. That way, at least some acorns survive and grow into oak trees. Many other plants grow lots of seeds. That makes it more likely that some will survive to grow into new plants.

Tough seeds

Palm trees are able to make only a few seeds (coconuts). The coconuts have such tough shells that all of them are likely to survive.

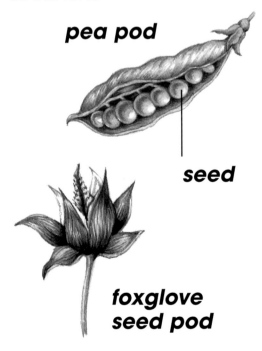

pea pod

seed

foxglove seed pod

All about seeds

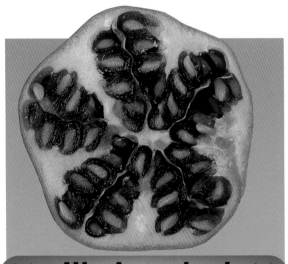

It's Amazing!

The pomegranate (above) fruit is from Asia. It has lots of seeds. In ancient times people thought it was a sign of new life. The seeds are blood red, so people also thought the fruit was a sign of death. Ancient Greeks told the story of Persephone, a girl who was kidnapped by the god of the underworld, Hades. She escaped, but Hades tricked her into eating six pomegranate seeds. She had to spend six months in the underworld each year— one month for each seed.

Spreading seeds

If seeds grew right next to their parent plant, they might get in the way of each other. So seeds need to be carried far away.

Some seeds are blown away by the wind. Some are washed away by water. Some are carried by animals. Some plants, like peas, have seed pods that burst open. When the pod bursts, the seeds are flung through the air.

Wind and water

Seeds spread by the wind are very light. Tiny poppy seeds are like this. Some bigger seeds have papery wings that help them stay in the air. That lets them be carried away. Maple and sycamore seeds have wings like this. The wings make the seed whirl in the air like a helicopter. Some seeds, like dandelions and thistles, have feathery hairs that catch in the wind and get blown along.

Seeds carried by water have waterproof shells. The large fruits of the water lily can float away. When they settle in mud, the seeds inside the fruits grow into new water lilies.

▼ Dandelions

A dandelion seed is in a tiny fruit with its own mini parachute. A light breeze catches the parachute and blows it away.

It's Amazing!

The tumbleweed is a plant that lives in the southwestern United States. When a tumbleweed spreads its seeds, it is not just the seeds that move. The whole plant moves. Each plant makes 20,000 to 50,000 papery seeds. When the seeds ripen. the tumbleweed's stem gets very weak. Soon, the weak stem is broken off by the wind. The wind then tumbles the plant along. The plant spreads seeds as it goes.

How seeds grow

A new plant begins life when a seed starts to grow, or germinate (sprout). The seed soaks up water and swells. The outer seed coat splits. Then the tiny plant inside starts to grow. As it grows, the new plant uses the seed's store of food.

Everything must be right for a seed to germinate. All seeds need water. Some need a lot of warmth or light, too. A few seeds grow only after they have been through a frost. Some seeds only grow after they are burned by fire.

Some seeds sit in the ground for many years before they start to grow. Such seeds are called dormant. In Canada, scientists were able to grow dormant seeds that had been buried in frozen ground for 10,000 years!

Try This!

You can grow your own seeds. Ask an adult to buy some mustard or radish seeds. Put some cotton balls in the bottom of a glass jar. Spray the cotton with a little water. Spread seeds on top. Put the jar in a dark place. Spray water on the seeds every few days. Then watch the plants grow.

▶ Sprouting seeds
Two washed-up coconuts have started to grow. There is little food on this beach, but the seeds contain enough food to sprout.

Seeds and animals

Seeds and animals rely on each other. Many seeds are spread by animals. Many animals eat seeds.

▼ Little hooks

The fruits that hold burr seeds are spread by animals. They are covered in hooks that catch on fur. The hooks gave people the idea for Velcro.

Some seeds themselves taste good to animals. They provide food. Other seeds are inside tasty fruit or nuts. Animals eat these fruit and nuts. But the seeds inside are tough, so they pass out in animal droppings. The seeds fall to the ground, ready to grow.

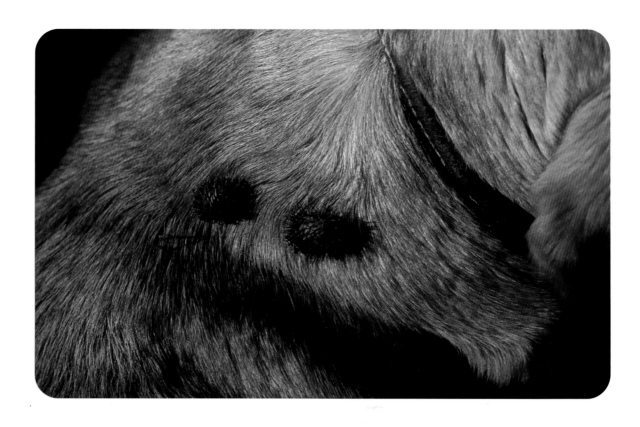

Animals spread seeds in other ways, too. Many seeds hitch a ride on animals. The fruits that hold the seeds of burdock and garden lawn weeds like goose-grass have hooks and spikes. These hooks and spikes catch on the fur of passing animals. Some seeds have sticky coats that stick to an animal. The fruit and seeds may be carried a long way before they fall off.

It's Amazing!

Some animals do not just carry seeds. They plant them, too! In fall, squirrels and jays gather nuts such as acorns. They do not eat the acorns at once. Instead, they bury them to eat in winter when there is not much food. But the animals often forget where they buried the acorns. So acorns are left planted in the ground ready to grow.

13

black noddy bird

The seeds of a pisonia plant catch on the bird's feathers.

Birds that eat seeds

Finches, doves, pigeons, parrots, and many other birds eat seeds. Seeds are very tough, so birds that eat seeds need strong beaks. Seed-eating birds all have short, thick beaks. These birds use their beaks like nutcrackers to crack the seeds open.

There are few seeds around in winter. So, from spring to fall, birds such as jays bury seeds. They save these seeds to dig up later during winter. Willow tits can bury a thousand seeds a day. Birds called nutcrackers might bury up to 30,000 seeds each year.

It's Amazing!

There are many kinds of finches, and each has a different beak. The shape of a finch's beak helps the bird eat its favorite seeds. Greenfinches have strong beaks for eating tough sunflower seeds. A hawfinch's beak is so strong it can crack a cherry pit. The tips of a crossbill's beak cross over. That helps it pull seeds out of pine cones.

greenfinch

Some birds store seeds in the ground. That can be good for a seed. If a bird forgets the seed, it is planted in the ground, ready to grow. Some woodpeckers drill holes in tree trunks to store seeds. Those seeds cannot grow!

▲ Acorn supply

The acorn woodpecker likes acorns very much. It makes little holes in tree trunks with its beak. Then it puts an acorn in each hole. That way, the bird has food when acorns are hard to find.

Animals that eat seeds

Some animals eat soft fruit with seeds inside, like apples and plums. The animal eats the soft flesh, and the seeds pass out in the animal's droppings.

Many tiny animals such as mice and squirrels eat hard seeds and nuts. Just as birds need tough beaks to eat seeds, these animals need strong teeth.

Mice have two sharp front teeth called incisors. Even though the teeth are tough, they are worn down by chewing on hard seeds. So the teeth keep growing all the time, just like human fingernails. The teeth of other animals stop growing once they are adults.

Animals with teeth that keep growing are called rodents. Mice, rats, and beavers are all rodents. The toughest teeth of all belong to a rodent called the agouti. The agouti is a rabbit-sized animal that lives in the forests of South America. Its teeth are so tough they can crack a brazil nut!

◀ Nuts for a mouse

For a wood mouse, fall is a time of plenty, as hazelnuts fall from trees. The mouse eats a few nuts but rolls most back to its nest to eat in winter. The seeds inside some of the nuts are left uneaten by the mouse. These can grow into hazel trees.

It's Amazing!

The seeds of many plants in southern Africa are planted in an unusual way. The seeds are coated with an oil that ants find very tasty. To get the oil, ants drag the seeds to their nests under the ground. The ants then chew the oil off the seeds. But they do not like the seed itself, so they leave it. The seed is then under the ground, ready to grow.

Seeds and people

Seeds can be good to eat. Grass seeds are the basic food of people all around the world.

Wheat, corn, oats, rye, barley, millet, and rice are all kinds of grasses called cereals. The seeds of cereals are called grains. The grains grow in clumps, or ears, at the top of the stems. People eat the seeds of these plants.

Farmers plant cereals every year. The cereals grow quickly, and soon have ears of grain. When the seeds are ripe,

the farmers cut down the grass and collect the grain. This is called harvesting.

Sometimes people eat cereals whole. Eating corn on the cob is eating sweet corn seeds whole. Sometimes grains are turned into flakes for breakfast cereals. Rice grains are cooked in water. People grind many grains to make flour. They use flour to make everything from bread to pasta and cakes.

◀ Harvest time
When wheat turns golden, the seeds are ripe. The farmer uses a machine to cut off the stems and harvest the grain.

It's Amazing!

More than half the people in the world eat rice as their main food. In some warm, wet places in Asia and Africa, many people eat little else besides rice. With enough water, rice can be grown and harvested two or three times a year. Most rice is grown in fields called paddies (above). The fields are flooded with water to help the rice grow.

19

Seeds for oils and spices

Seeds may look dry, but most contain oil. People crush the seeds to collect the oil. Nearly all the cooking oils people use come from seeds. Sunflower oil is made from crushed sunflower seeds. Corn oil is made from crushed corn seeds (kernels). Olive oil is made from crushed olive pits (seeds).

People use oil from seeds for many other things besides cooking. Castor oil was once only used for curing a stomachache. Now it is used to make plastics, cloth, paints, makeup, and even glue. Oil from rape seeds keeps machines running smoothly. Linseed oil is used to protect wood.

It's Amazing!

Recently, scientists found out how to use sunflowers to keep the world clean. Oil from the seeds (right) can be used to make a gas called hydrogen. Cars can burn this instead of gasoline. Unlike burning gasoline, burning hydrogen does not pollute (dirty) the air. Scientists hope cars in the future will run on the seeds made by huge fields of sunflowers.

rice
(grass
seeds)

green
lentils

rice

People grind up some kinds of seeds to make spices. Spices make food tasty. Carraway, pepper, coriander, and mustard are just some of the spices made from seeds.

▲ Spices and seeds
Each of these bags is filled with a different spice or seed. The red spice is ground-up seeds of the paprika plant. It tastes very hot.

Cotton seeds

Cotton seeds are very, very fluffy. People use this fluff to make clothes. The seeds grow inside a pod called a boll. When the seeds are ripe, the boll splits open. Then out bursts a ball of fluff covering the seeds.

People pick the fluff balls by hand or with machines. They split the fluff, or "lint," from the seeds. The lint is twisted together to make long strings called yarn. Yarn is woven into cotton cloth. Clothes are made from the cloth.

◄ Cotton balls
These white clumps are fluffy open cotton bolls. There are about 30 seeds in each boll. Each seed is covered in fluff. The fluff helps the wind spread the seeds around.

Glossary

acorn the nut of an oak tree.

boll the seed pod of a cotton plant.

burr a prickly seed that sticks to animal fur and bird feathers.

cereal a grass plant with seeds that can be eaten.

dormant in a life stage during which little seems to happen, like a seed before it sprouts.

embryo the young, tiny plant that grows inside a seed.

fruit the part of a plant that contains its seeds.

germinate to sprout from a seed into a plant.

grain a seed that can be eaten, like the seeds of cereals.

incisor the sharp front teeth of a small, seed-eating animal.

nut a fruit with a hard shell.

pod the oval-shaped part of a plant that contains seeds.

rodent a small furry animal with long incisors. Mice, rats, and beavers are rodents.

seed coat the tough outer layer of a seed.

Find out more

Books

Sally Morgan. *Flowers, Fruits and Seeds.* New York: Chrysalis, 2004.

Patricia Whitehouse. *Seeds (Read and Learn).* Chicago: Heinemann Library, 2002.

Web sites

The Great Plant Escape
www.urbanext.uiuc.edu/gpe

Kids Valley Garden
www.raw-connections.com/garden

Index